Danny Boyle and the Underland

Copyright © 2001 William Graham
All rights reserved.

ISBN 1-58898-566-0

Danny Boyle and the Underland

William Graham

greatunpublished.com
Title No. 566
2001

Danny Boyle and the Underland

Preface

The Murphys had all the windows open in their house. It was a steamy summer night and they didn't have air conditioning. Window fans buzzed like small airplane engines in their bedroom windows.

At three o'clock in the morning Mr. Murphy awoke. He thought he heard wood cracking. He went downstairs carrying a golf club, thinking that a burglar might be trying to break into his garage. He turned on the light above the back porch. No one was there, except for a raccoon that had been trying to pry open the garbage can.

Mr. Murphy returned to bed. Mrs. Murphy hadn't heard a thing. She was still snoring like a bear when Mr. Murphy drifted off to sleep again.

Just as Mr. Murphy was dreaming about hitting a hole in one, his house shook, as if there was an earthquake. But this was Rivertown. There were no earthquakes in Rivertown. He bolted from his bed to his bedroom window just in time to see his neighbor's house sink into the ground as if a giant hand was pulling it down. Plaster and brick dust drifted through the soft glare of streetlights.

"Thank goodness the O'Donnells are away on vacation," Mr. Murphy thought to himself. "No one will be injured."

He tried to awaken his wife out of her deep sleep.

"Francine!" he yelled. "Get up! The O'Donnells' house collapsed. Just like the others."

"Is it time to get up already? Just a few more minutes," Mrs. Murphy said.

Rather than dealing with his sleepy wife, Mr. Murphy called the police and reported another house collapse in Rivertown.

To Jacqueline

Chapter 1

Houses were collapsing mysteriously in Rivertown, a small community perched on sandstone bluffs overlooking the Mississippi River. The mystery had been going on for almost one hundred years. Sometimes several houses would collapse in a year. And then several years would go by and everything would be back to normal. But just as suddenly, houses would begin to crumble and fall into large holes once again. Many families in Rivertown could tell tales of collapsed houses dating back several generations. The citizens of Rivertown couldn't understand what was happening. And when people don't understand something, rumors begin to grow and spread.

Some people said that old wells or lead mines were collapsing. Some blamed the devil. And there were even a few who believed that aliens from another planet were to blame. In reality, no one knew the reason for sure. All they knew was this: One moment their neighbor's house would be standing and then it would be sinking into the ground, disappearing into a large hole. Wood cracking. Dust rising into the air. A family's possessions lost.

But there was yet another side to this mystery. The morning after a collapse, most of the parts of a house would be gone. The pile of wood, brick, or stone vanished, as if it had been sucked right into the ground. Furniture was gone. Lights and light bulbs were nowhere to be found. Sometimes even cars and trucks disappeared.

But that still wasn't the end to the mystery. From the days when Rivertown first was wired for electricity there had been sudden and inexplicable losses of power. There would be no thunderstorms or tornadoes. No strong winds. Just sudden darkness. People kept blaming the power company. But the power company couldn't understand what was happening either. After a while, the people of Rivertown began to accept things. They even began to joke about it.

"Maybe we've got ourselves some giant ants living underneath us," the mayor said.

Some families left Rivertown out of fear. But most people stayed. Most people who were born in Rivertown died there. It was just that kind of place. They liked Rivertown. People thought it was a lovely place to live, all things considered. But even mothers and fathers, grandmothers and grandfathers, aunts and uncles, all who had lived in Rivertown for generations, sometimes grew quiet at night. When everyone was asleep and the streets were empty, they sat wondering and worrying about what was really happening in their quiet town that looked down on the broad, muddy Mississippi River.

Chapter 2

Danny Boyle's baseball cap and T-shirt were drenched in sweat. He was pushing his bike up Mercy Street on a blistering summer day when the concrete and the blacktop were so hot you could almost feel your skin begin to boil.

Danny was twelve years old. He had lived in Rivertown all of his life. He was short and skinny. His arms and legs looked like the narrow branches of a young tree that had just been planted. His brown sweaty hair dipped over his black wireframe glasses.

Danny's Uncle Albert lived on Mercy Street. Unfortunately for Danny, Uncle Albert lived at the very top of Mercy Street, which was so steep that cars didn't even try to reach the top in the winter.

"A street named Mercy," Danny thought. "On a day like today the name sounds pretty funny."

Uncle Albert lived in a house that was painted an ugly shade of green. Or at least that was what Danny's father—who was Uncle Albert's brother—had told Danny many times.

The steamy air was filled with the high-pitched sound of cicadas. Danny always thought it seemed hotter when cicadas started making noise. Danny thought they sounded like thousands of miniature fire truck sirens.

At the top of the hill, Danny stopped to catch his breath. With his T-shirt, he wiped off the sweat that was beginning to drip into his eyes and mouth. He could taste the salt. He wanted a cold drink, but he doubted that Uncle Albert would have any sodas. He knew that his uncle preferred beer, a lot of beer. This is why his parents never spoke too kindly of Uncle Albert. Danny's father called Uncle Albert a lazy drunk who always hung out at the White Stag Tap. But Uncle Albert had always been kind to Danny. Danny liked his stories about leprechauns and dragons and other mythical creatures of Ireland and England.

Danny set his bike against the side of the house and peered in the through the screen door. He could see his uncle sleeping on a bed in the front room. An old rusted fan was running in the corner, blowing hot air around the room.

Uncle Albert never slept in his bedroom on the second floor. As long as Danny could remember, Uncle Albert slept in his front room in an old iron frame bed with a sagging mattress.

"Uncle Albert, Uncle Albert," Danny said. "It's me, Danny. Wake up."

Uncle Albert began to groan and stir from his sleep.

"Who is it?" he asked, peeling his sweat-soaked undershirt from his body and sitting upright.

"It's me, Danny."

"Danny? Danny, my boy. Come in. Come on in," Uncle Albert said in his rapid-fire delivery. Uncle Albert spoke very quickly. It had taken Danny a while to learn to understand what he was saying. But even though Danny didn't hear every word that Uncle Albert spoke, he heard enough to figure out what he meant.

Danny entered through the front screen door that slammed loudly behind him.

"I've got to fix that door one of these days," Uncle Albert said. He had been saying the same thing for as long as Danny could remember. The door always had slammed shut too loudly.

The heat was stifling. He sat in an old brown chair in front of the fan, while his uncle sat upright in his bed. Danny liked the feel of the breeze on his sweaty T-shirt.

"Get yourself some water," Uncle Albert said. "It's a scorcher today."

"No thanks. I'll be all right," Danny said. The truth was that

Danny didn't want to drink out of one of Uncle Albert's dirty glasses.

"How did you get here?" Uncle Albert asked.

"On my bike," Danny said.

"On a day like today? You should stay inside where it's cool," Uncle Albert said, taking a sip from a bottle of beer that was sitting next to his bed. Danny wondered if it was warm or cold.

"I just wanted to come and say hello," Danny said. "Well, that's not the only reason. I wanted you to tell me again about your theory for the house collapses. There have been quite a few recently. And I would like to investigate things myself. It will make the summer more interesting."

"But I thought you had little league to keep you busy," Uncle Albert said.

"I do. But that's so predictable. I like some adventure in my life. Rivertown is so predictable," Danny said.

"I happen to like routine. Keeps things simple," Uncle Albert said, stretching his limbs like a cat that had just awoken from an afternoon nap.

"But if you think you know why the houses are collapsing you should try to prove your theory," Danny said.

"That would take too much work. And I don't have time for that," Uncle Albert said. "Besides, whether I'm proved right or wrong will make no difference. The houses will still disappear. It's Rivertown's curse. I've told you all this before."

"And I'm the only one who doesn't think you're crazy. Isn't that true?" Danny said.

"You are a true believer, my boy. That you are. A true believer. Not like my brother, who never had time for anything that wasn't logical," Uncle Albert said.

"I'm logical. Most of the time. And I still believe you," Danny said.

"Thanks, my boy. Thanks," Uncle Albert said, taking another long swig of beer."

"So you think that I could find the entrance to the cave where the outsiders were banished?" Danny asked.

"'Banished,'" Uncle Albert said. "Where are you learning these words?"

"I read a lot," said Danny.

"Well, if you're such a good reader you also know the word 'condemned,'" Uncle Albert said. "Yep, 'condemned' is the better word to describe what happened over one hundred years ago."

"There were the robberies," Danny said.

"That's right. And the outbreak of influenza. Followed by a terrible drought," Uncle Albert said.

"People blamed the wanderers."

"Blamed them for everything. When all they were looking for was jobs, food, and shelter for their families."

"There was a fire."

"Ten people died in the music hall."

"Twelve," Danny said. "Don't you remember? It was twelve. They blamed the wanderers for starting the fire.

"No evidence."

"Only rumor."

"People called them disciples of evil"

"Condemned thirty people to be sealed in a cave rather than be given a fair trial," Danny said, reciting the facts from memory. He had heard Uncle Albert tell the story dozens of times over the years. The best part was about to come. The part that made the hairs on Danny's arms stand up like they did during a lightning storm.

Uncle Albert then bent over as close as he could to Danny and continued the story by whispering: "Before they were sealed in the cave, the leader of the wanderers cast a curse on the people of Rivertown. The curse was that one day Rivertown would disappear into the ground with him. People just thought he was deranged."

"But maybe he wasn't," Danny said.

"You can't take curses lightly," Uncle Albert said. "Do so at your own risk."

"At your own risk," Danny echoed. Then and there Danny decided that this would be the summer when he would finally try to find the truth about the legend of the wanderers before his house disappeared into the ground.

Chapter 3

After returning from Uncle Albert's, Danny immediately went over to his best friend Chip Zumhoffer's house. Chip, like Danny, was twelve years old. But Chip was stockier and had close-cropped blond hair, like the kind soldiers get when they join the army.

Danny and Chip went to the basement where Chip had a playroom that had been built by Chip's father, who was a carpenter. Chip knew alot about all kinds of tools and about how to make things. Danny liked that about Chip.

Danny had often told Chip about Uncle Albert's story of the wanderers. Chip had always been more skeptical of the story than Danny.

"Do you believe him?" Chip asked.

"Yes. Do you?" Danny said.

"I don't know. It sounds crazy," Chip said.

"Then how do you explain what's been going on?"

"I don't know. We're just kids. We're supposed to have fun. Play baseball. Build treehouses and stuff like that," Chip said, shrugging his shoulders.

"But we've done all that. And I'm kinda bored by it. Aren't you?"

"No. Not really,"

"Then I guess you wouldn't be interested in trying to find the wanderers by going into that big cave in the quarry?" Danny said.

Chip was silent. He had listened to Danny's other ideas about traveling down the Amazon, climbing Mount Everest, and a dozen other adventures that never happened. Chip thought that this would just be another wild idea that would come and go.

"You always say that you want to go on some big adventure, but you always chicken out," Chip said.

"I know," Danny said. "But this time it's different. This time I'm actually going to do it, whether you come along or not."

Chip had always looked out for Danny, whom he had known since kindergarten. Danny was smart and nice, but was a dreamer. Chip tried to keep him out of trouble.

"Let's pack our backpacks tonight with some food, a flashlight, and some warm clothes and meet in the old quarry at dawn," Danny said. " If there is something going on under Rivertown, I bet we can find out."

Chip had always liked small, dark places. So going into a cave sounded appealing. He once lived for several days in his closet until his mother told him to stop. He had gone a few yards into one of the quarry's caves before, but never deep into one.

"OK," said Chip. "Let's do it."

"Dawn tomorrow," said Danny.

"I'll be there," Chip said.

Danny was very pleased. He ran back to his house, shut his bedroom door from the prying eyes of his parents and his little sister Melinda, and began to prepare for his journey beneath the streets of Rivertown.

Chapter 4

The sound of a freight train awoke Danny at four o'clock in the morning. On clear summer nights in Rivertown, the blast of a train whistle, the rhythmic clack of the wheels on the iron rails, and the dull rumble of the diesel engine carried for miles across the still air from the train bridge crossing the Mississippi River to Danny's house on Blackhawk Lane.

A street lamp sat outside his window. It gave him just enough light to check his clock. When he saw the time, Danny launched himself from his bed, grabbed his glasses, and looked out of his window. Chip wasn't there yet. He must have overslept, Danny thought.

In his backpack, Danny had placed a sweatshirt, a jacket, and gloves because caves were cold and damp. He also had a flashlight and, if necessary, some candles that he found in the kitchen. He hoped his Mom wouldn't notice that they were gone. As for food, he wasn't sure how long he was going to be gone so he wasn't sure what to take. He packed small orange juice and milk cartons, two water bottles, some chocolate chip cookies, a couple of bananas, and a peanut butter-and-jelly sandwich. He declared himself ready. He believed that Chip would be arriving soon.

Danny dressed himself quietly. He put on jeans, his favorite blue T-shirt, tennis shoes, and his black Rivertown Roughnecks baseball hat. He waited for Chip. He waited and waited until it was four-thirty. No Chip. He waited until five o'clock. No Chip. All Danny heard were the sounds of big black crows making a racket in the trees.

By five-thirty Danny had to go to the bathroom. He opened his bedroom door softly, but the hinges squeaked. At this time of the morning, Danny thought, everything sounds like an explosion of dynamite. He stopped, waiting to see if either of his parents heard the noise. There was no sound from behind their bedroom door.

Danny was almost to the bathroom when he heard a voice that made his entire body twitch violently, like when you come around a corner not expecting to find anybody there but someone really is there. It's like being hit by a lightning bolt.

"Why are you dressed already? Where are you going? What are you doing?" asked his 10-year-old sister Melinda. Melinda had been advanced two grades in her school. So even though she was younger than Danny, she and Danny were in the same class, much to Danny's annoyance. She always liked to know what was going on and why. Her parents and teachers always called her "gifted." Danny just called her a "pain."

"I'm just going to the bathroom," Danny said. "Are you blind? And what are you doing up so early?" Danny whispered in his stern big brother voice.

Melinda was not deterred. "I'm not blind. People don't put on their jeans and a baseball hat just to go to the bathroom," she said, with hands on her hips and her head cocked to one side. Her red hair was matted in a ball on the right side of her head. "Something is going on. And I want to know."

"Shhh. Be quiet. You'll wake Mom and Dad, and then we'll both get in trouble. I have a little league game this morning and I just couldn't sleep. OK? Now just let me go to the bathroom," he said.

"Some story. I don't believe you. You can tell me the real reason later. Or I'll find out myself. I have to go, too," Melinda said.

"You can wait," Danny said, closing the door.

Back in his room, Danny saw the sunrise but did not see Chip. Too tired to wait anymore, he went back to his bed, burrowed under the covers, and fell asleep. He dreamed that a giant crow had swooped down and captured him in its claws.

Chapter 5

Later that morning, Danny said a quick goodbye to his parents after breakfast. He avoided Melinda's annoying questions. He went to Chip's house. Chip's mother said that Chip had left about a thirty minutes ago. Danny knew where Chip had gone—to the treehouse that he and Chip had built.

Their treehouse was about one-half mile from their parents' houses on Blackhawk Street, deep in the thick woods that lay between the abandoned sandstone quarry and a city golf course. Danny supplied the design and Chip supplied most of the labor, tools, and wood, which he borrowed from his father.

They found a tree whose trunk branched off into four directions, leaving a perfect square space between the trunks in which to construct their multistory treehouse. Their treehouse sat about ten feet off the ground. They nailed wooden steps into one the trunks. The steps led to the roof deck of the treehouse. On the deck, there was a door in the ceiling of the treehouse through which one descended into the main room of the treehouse. But a person could also climb higher from the roof deck to a small lookout platform perched in the branches.

The treehouse had two screened windows for light and ventilation. Wooden shutters kept out the rain. Their furniture consisted of two old wooden chairs and a table. They hung a camping lamp from the ceiling for light. There was enough space for two boys to lie in sleeping bags on the floor.

Danny plowed through the path to the treehouse, twisting and breaking branches along the way. He was angry that Chip had not shown up that morning. Chip sat in the lookout perch and saw Danny coming.

"Hey, where were you this morning?" Danny yelled to Chip. "We had everything planned."

"I just couldn't do it," Chip said from high above in the branches. "It sounded good while we were talking yesterday, but then I thought about actually searching for some mysterious people who live underground I decided it was a stupid idea."

"Stupid? What are you talking about? It would be an adventure. And you always liked going into caves," Danny said as he climbed to the roof deck.

"I do. I do," Chip said, scrambling down to meet Danny. "But the more I thought about it lying in bed last night the more I thought that it might be dangerous. What if your Uncle Albert is right? What if there are people living beneath Rivertown? If we find them, they might kill us."

"So you're afraid? Afraid of a little adventure?" Danny said in a mocking tone.

"Maybe a little. Aren't you?" Chip said.

"No. Not at all. I'm not afraid. Great explorers cannot be afraid of danger or what might be around the next corner," Danny said. "I'll go by myself if you won't come with me."

Chip didn't say anything. He thought for a moment about letting Danny go by himself. But then he decided that he couldn't let his best friend descend into the caves without his help.

"OK. I'll come with you," Chip said.

"Great!" Danny said. He had hoped that Chip would not let back out on him.

"But let's make a deal," Chip said. "Let's give ourselves one day. If we don't find any signs of the wanderers in one day, then we'll come back and it'll be our secret."

"One day?" Danny said.

"One day."

"You're not going to leave me waiting like you did this morning," Danny said.

"I'll be there tomorrow morning at dawn," Chip said.

"Just make sure that you pack some useful stuff. Like rope. We might need some rope, but I don't have any at home," Danny said.

"There's some in our garage. And we should probably bring our bike helmets," Chip said. "There might be falling rocks."

"A bike helmet. That's what I forgot to pack. Good idea," Danny said, angry at himself for forgetting such an important piece of equipment. He thought of himself as a careful planner.

"Do you'll think we'll see bats?" Chip asked.

"We might. I see them flying around at sunset. They're looking for insects you know," Danny said. "They might live in the quarry cave."

"I guess we'll find out," Chip said.

"I hope we find out a lot of things, Danny said.

Chip and Danny spent the rest of the day sitting on the roof deck of their treehouse planning their adventure as the blistering summer sun poured through the thick green leaves.

Chapter 6

The heat broke during the night. Storms hit Rivertown like a big fist. Sharp cracks of lightning scarred the night sky. But Danny slept right through most of the storm. He found storms comforting. Unlike some of his friends at school, thunder and lightning never scared him.

It was still drizzling the next morning as Danny awoke. Dark clouds hung like wet blankets from the sky. But Danny didn't care about the weather. He was prepared for his adventure.

He acted as normally as possible that morning. He told his parents that he and Chip were going to spend the day playing in Chip's basement since it was too wet to play baseball. His mother reminded him to return home for lunch.

When his mother was downstairs in the laundry room, Danny yelled a quick "Goodbye" and ran out of the house with his full backpack so that he mother wouldn't see what he was carrying. Melinda had also left earlier to visit her friend Audrey who lived two blocks away, so Danny also avoided running into her. Everything was going as planned.

Chip and Danny had agreed to meet in the woods near their treehouse and then go together to the old quarry.

This time Chip was there. He was ready. He had remembered to bring rope. And they both had their bike helmets tucked into their packs.

They started walking through the wet woods. The trees and

bushes were drooping from the night's heavy rain. The trail on which they walked was soggy and muddy. The rain had finally stopped, but the sky was still cloudy. And it was beginning to get hot again. "This is what the Amazon jungle must feel like," Danny thought. They took off their jackets as the heat and humidity began to rise. Their shoes were caked in heavy brown mud.

After about thirty minutes, they emerged from the woods and entered a giant limestone pit that had been blasted and carved away over many years by the quarrymen. Puddles of water of various sizes and shapes were scattered across the rock floor, which was as long as three baseball fields. Stone terraces rose sharply from the floor, like stands in a baseball stadium. The cave that Danny and Chip planned to explore was on the third terrace, about forty feet above where they were standing. No one else was there. Chip yelled "Hello" and his voice echoed around the sandstone walls.

They carefully climbed up the slippery rock path that was covered with crumbled and discarded limestone chunks. They had climbed this trail before to sit at the mouth of the cave on hot days. Cool, moist air streamed up from the deep recesses of the earth. It was a natural air conditioner. Even on the hottest days, Danny and Chip could sit in the cave and see their breath floating in the air, just like it did in the middle of winter. But until now, they had never ventured into the cave itself.

After Danny and Chip reach the third terrace, they looked down at where they had come, marveling at the view of the entire quarry. They looked in the mouth of the cave. Small streams of water dripped from the top of the entrance, making muddy puddles on the floor of the cave.

"You're not going to turn back now, are you?" Danny asked Chip.

"I came this far, didn't I?" Chip replied.

Just at that moment, a yell came from the bottom of the quarry pit. "Danny. Chip. I know you're up there. I can see you from here."

"It's your sister Melinda. What's she doing here?" Chip said, spotting Melinda on the floor of the quarry far beneath them. She was wearing blue overalls, pink sneakers, and a white baseball hat, pulled down over her forehead. "Now everything is ruined, and we're going to get into trouble."

"I thought she was at her friend Audrey's house. She wasn't at home when I left this morning," Danny explained.

"She must have been spying on you," Chip said.

"She's been following us all morning," Danny said. He should have had a contingency plan for this. He knew Melinda was capable of being devious. "I'm going to kill her!"

He yelled back to Melinda. "Go back. You're not supposed to be here. You know that. I'm going to tell Mom and Dad."

"Go ahead. You'll get into as much trouble as me," Melinda said. "I knew you were up to something yesterday morning. You're supposed to be at Chip's house. I heard you say that this morning. So you lied to Mom and Dad. Do you want me to tell them that? I'm coming up."

"No. Stay where you are!" Danny yelled again.

"No. I'm coming up. And what are you going to do about it? Nothing!" she said, as she began scrambling up the path to the cave.

"So what are we going to do now?" Chip asked Danny.

"Let me think a minute," Danny said, pacing nervously as he looked down at his sister's progress up the rocky path. "We're just going to have to let her join us, if she's not afraid. Maybe I can scare her into returning."

"Scare Melinda?" Chip said. "Good luck."

Melinda was breathing heavily and sweating when she arrived at the cave. The sun had begun to emerge from the clouds. It was going to be another blistering day. "So what's going on?" she asked, her hands on her hips.

"If you really want to know, here goes," Danny said. He began telling Uncle Albert's tale about the wanderers living underneath Rivertown. Melinda stood silently and listened intently to every word.

"So this adventure could be scary and dangerous," Danny concluded. "Who knows what we might find. So you still want to come with us?"

"Yes. I'm not scared. Uncle Albert was probably just making the whole thing up anyway. You know he likes to drink a lot of beers. And you believed him. But then again, you always were more gullible than me. I bet all we'll find in that musty old cave is a few bats," Melinda said. She liked using big words like "gullible" to show everyone why she skipped ahead two grades.

"But you don't have the right equipment," Danny said. "We've planned this journey carefully. Look, we have food, flashlights, rope, even bike helmets. You don't have equipment."

"I don't plan on staying underground for long. Besides, Chip will share. Won't you, Chip?" Melinda said.

"Yeah, sure," Chip said, grinning foolishly.

"Nice going," Chip. "You're supposed to be on my side."

"So are we going in or just standing here," Melinda said. "It's getting hot out here."

"OK. OK. We're going. All of us. Just don't get in our way," Danny snarled at Melinda. "Let's put on our helmets, turn on our flashlights, and head in," Danny said.

Melinda thought Danny and Chip looked silly wearing their bike helmets. But she stopped herself from firing a sarcastic remark. She got what she had wanted. She was joining them on their adventure. She decided to be quiet for a while as she followed her big brother and Chip into the quarry cave.

Chapter 7

After about twenty feet, the cave became too small for Danny, Chip, and Melinda to stand upright. They began crawling on the cave's muddy floor. They soon became caked in cool mud.

The passage became smaller and began to slope downward. Danny scraped his hand against the side wall. He wanted to cry out from the pain, but he didn't. He didn't want to show any emotion but resolve to Chip and Melinda.

Danny also wondered how he would explain his dirty, wet clothes and the wound on his hand to his parents. He decided that he had to stop thinking about such things and concentrate on where he was going.

The journey was becoming more difficult. They all began to think that they would be stuck in the cave and lost forever. Danny was in the lead, pointing his flashlight into the total darkness. He could see nothing except the rock all around him.

Melinda was behind him. Chip brought up the rear, making sure than Melinda was always in the beam of his flashlight. He was excited but also nervous. Chip and Danny had never been this deep in a cave before. He wasn't prepared for how cold and cramped it was.

"Well, I don't see any secret or scary people down here. I don't even see any bats. So let's just go back," Melinda said.

"Be quiet," Danny said. "We've barely begun to look. Just because we don't find something doesn't mean it doesn't exist. The

Inca's sacred city of Machu Picchu wasn't discovered for hundreds of years, you know."

"As a matter of fact, I did know that," Melinda said.

Before Danny could respond, he stopped abruptly. "Look. Look. Here's some writing on the wall," he said.

Danny pointed his flashlight to the wall, where scrawled on the rock were the words: "Remember the forgotten. Triumph to the Wanderers! Their glory will arise from the underneath."

"The Wanderers," Chip said. "That's what your Uncle Albert said they were called. They must have written that."

"You don't know that," Melinda scoffed. "Anyone could have written that. It could be a prank, a hoax."

"A what?" Chip said.

"She's saying that it could be fake," Danny said.

"I'm saying that it's probably fake," Melinda corrected him.

"Well, there's only one way to find out. And that's to keep going," Danny said. "Or are you to afraid to continue, Melinda?"

"Let's go," Melinda said.

"Chip, what about you?" Danny said.

Chip knew that Danny was going to ask him that question. Chip was afraid, but he wasn't going to admit it.

"Let's keep going. Maybe the passage will get bigger. I'm getting cramped where we are," Chip said,

They continued crawling downward for another fifteen minutes. They began to notice that the passage had become bigger. After a few feet, the passage was once again large enough for them to all stand up. They were relieved to stretch their legs and backs. They stopped at the place where two passages diverged and ate cookies and drank water.

"So which way do we go, Mr. Navigator?" Melinda said to Danny.

"Just give me time to think," Danny said.

"Look," Chip said. "I see lights coming toward us."

They stood frozen, wondering if they should stay or run, yell or remain silent. Their hearts raced. Blood pounded in their heads.

They felt that mysterious tingle on the back of their necks that you get when you think someone might be in a dark room but you can't see anything.

"Quick, turn off the flashlights and don't say a word," Danny ordered. They crouched down together and stared at the approaching lights.

They were suddenly tackled from behind. They all screamed as loud as they could. The screeching sounds of their voices echoed off the walls of the cave.

They couldn't see who had attacked them, but they could smell something awful. They punched and poked at their attackers, who yelled at them, telling them to be quiet. Danny grabbed a rock with his right hand and struck one of his attackers, who yelped in pain. Danny punched over and over again with the rock. He yelled at Chip and Melinda to do the same, but he didn't know exactly where they were. It was chaos in the darkness.

The attack was over as abruptly as it had begun. Danny sat up against a wall, checking to see if he was hurt. Other than being covered in mud, he was unharmed. He pulled the flashlight out of his pocket, hoping that it wasn't broken. He switched the light on. Danny sighed in relief that he would be able to see. He moved the beam of light around the passage, searching for Chip and Melinda. He spotted Chip a few feet away, bleeding from a cut on his head. Danny quickly crawled to him.

"Are you all right?" Danny asked.

"I think so, but I'll have a big goose egg on my head," Chip said. "Someone ripped my helmet off."

"Melinda. Where's Melinda?" Danny said, moving his light frantically around the passage. Melinda was gone.

"They've taken Melinda," Danny said.

"Do you think the Wanderers have her?" Chip said.

"It must be them. Uncle Albert was right. The legend is true. We have to find her. Pick up your stuff and let's go. I see some tracks in the mud that we can follow," Danny said urgently. "Come on."

"Maybe we should just go back and tell our parents and call the police. This isn't fun anymore. We should go back," Chip urged.

"Do you think our parents or the police would believe us? And it would be hours before the police could send anyone down here. We can begin searching now," Danny said. "I'll go myself if you won't come."

"And then you'd be lost. OK. Let's go," Chip said, worried that they were making a big mistake. He put his backpack on and switched on his flashlight.

Danny and Chip followed the tracks left in the muddy passage that began to slope downward sharply. They each held a big rock in their right hands in case they had to fight again.

"Why can't I just say 'no' to Danny just once?" Chip thought as he rubbed the huge welt on his head with his hand.

Chapter 8

Danny and Chip descended deeper into the core of the cave. They noticed many passages branching out from the one in which they crawled. They didn't know which passage to take because the tracks that they had hoped to follow had disappeared. The cave floor, which had been muddy, became smooth and dry. They had no signs to follow. So, to find their way back, Danny began scratching marks shaped like arrows in the cave walls with the rock that he carried. But knowing how to return to the cave entrance was of no comfort to Danny.

Danny looked at his watch. It was almost six o'clock in the afternoon. His parents and Chip's parents would now be wondering where they were. He thought about how worried his Mom and Dad must be. Maybe they thought that he had been kidnapped or had injured himself. Well, Danny thought, Melinda had been kidnapped, but not by someone from their world. If he didn't find Melinda and return safely, no one would believe his story.

"Danny," Chip said. "I can't go on much farther. I'm getting hungry and my feet hurt."

"OK. We can rest a few minutes. I'm getting tired, too," Danny said. "Let's stop here and eat."

Danny and Chip ate their sandwiches and drank from their water bottles. They were too exhausted to speak. Except for a few remaining candy bars and cookies they had each brought, their food was nearly gone. Neither one had planned for an overnight stay in the caves. Danny knew that they couldn't search for much longer, but he didn't want to admit this to Chip.

As they sat against the walls of the cave, they both fell asleep. Danny dreamed that he was flying in a spaceship to Mars. Chip dreamed that he was back in his warm bed at home.

Danny was aroused from his deep sleep by a bright light shining in his face. "Chip, get that out of my eyes," Danny said.

"I am not your companion Chip," a voice said from behind the blinding light. "I am in the service of Renegade Ralph."

Danny's body tensed and he tried to move, but he was held down by the hands of three strangers whom he could not see.

"Don't be afraid," the stranger said. "We are not here to harm you. We are here to help you and your friend find the little girl who was stolen from you."

"Who are you? Chip! Chip, are you there?" Danny yelled.

"Danny, I'm right here. I'm fine. I'm OK," Chip said.

"Let me go," Danny said, struggling to break free.

"Of course," the stranger replied, nodding to his companions who promptly released Danny.

"My name is Harold, and this is Sam and Daniel," Harold said, introducing his friends, who nodded politely.

"Who are you? Are you the Wanderers?" Danny asked.

"That title is an old one, given to us by others. We are just who we are. Like you. But we'll have time for explanation later. I promise you. But now you must come with us because the Grand Master's raiding parties are on the move. We need to go quickly for the safety of all of us."

"You will help us find my sister Melinda?" Danny said.

"Yes, but no more talking. We must go now," Harold said anxiously.

Danny had no choice but to follow and trust Harold. This could be the only way he and Chip could find Melinda and return to their homes safely. Danny and Chip gathered their backpacks and followed the three silent strangers into the darkness.

Chapter 9

Harold and his companions led Danny and Chip through a maze of tunnels with their old-fashioned lanterns that Danny once saw in an antique shop. Danny also noticed that Harold, Sam, and Daniel were dressed in a hodgepodge of clothes—baggy wool pants, ill-fitting boots, ripped plaid jackets with vests, and shirts with no collars.

A few of the passages were large enough for the group to stand in, whereas others were so narrow that everyone had to crawl. No one spoke.

In one tunnel that descended sharply, Harold said quietly that they were almost to the great cavern. Danny emerged from the tunnel and saw that he was on a narrow trail near the ceiling of a magnificent cavern that was illuminated by what appeared to be electric lights. Far below him was a dark body of water. In the distance were the lights of a small village jammed up against the wet, dark rock.

"You have electricity?" Danny asked.

"Yes," Harold replied. "Our ancestors discovered many generations ago how to bring the sun into our world. But please be very quiet as we go down to the village. We do not want to anger the demon who lives in the lake."

Danny and Chip looked at each other. Neither one was going to make the mistake of uttering a word. Instead, they concentrated on keeping their balance on the narrow trail's slippery, loose rocks.

They were very tired. They just wanted food and a warm place to sleep. They hoped these treats would be in store for them when they arrived at the village. In reality, they had been away from their homes for a day but it seemed like forever.

Danny and Chip followed Harold, Sam, and Daniel along the shore of the lake. Eventually they connected to a path that led them to the village.

"We are almost there," Harold said, flashing a brief smile at Danny and Chip.

Danny could begin to see the village more clearly. It had a few dozen small but neat homes built in a style from the 1940s and 1950s, like the kind his grandparents had. Many houses had wooden siding that was faded or peeled. Each house had a small wooden porch with a light hanging above the front door inviting people to come in. Each house was separated from another by small stone fences. Danny noticed that there were no grass, trees, or any living plant. In fact, nobody was even out walking. All the houses were dark except for their small porch lights.

"Where is everybody?" Chip whispered to Danny. But it was Harold who answered.

"It is very late. You will meet many people tomorrow. But now it is time for you to rest," he said.

They were heading to one house that was perched above the others on an outcropping of stone.

"This is where Renegade Ralph lives. Here you will find food and a place to sleep," Harold said.

Sam and Daniel offered to carry Danny and Chip's backpacks. They walked ahead and opened the door to the large house. Once inside, Danny and Chip could not see much, because the lights were kept off. Their escorts used their lanterns to lead them up creaky wooden stairs to a small room that had two small beds. In between the beds was a small wooden table. Hanging from the ceiling was a single light bulb. In a small adjoining room Danny saw an old toilet and a wash stand. He wondered if they worked.

"Please, " Harold said. "Make yourself comfortable. We will be back shortly with something for you to eat and drink."

True to his word, Harold returned with two small sandwiches and glasses of water. Chip was about to complain about the food—he wanted a Coke—but Danny poked him before he could utter a word.

"We will return for you in a few hours. Rest is what you need now. We will have a chance to talk more tomorrow," Harold said, shutting the door.

Danny and Chip ate their sandwiches and drank their water. Then they washed the mud off of themselves as best they could. They lay down in their beds, which had iron frames and large, warm comforters that appeared to be hand sown.

They were too tired to be scared. But they were bewildered by the many things they had seen and experienced in just one day. For a few minutes they listened to the muffled voices that they heard through the walls. Soon, however, they both burrowed under the covers and fell asleep. Chip dreamed that he was back home. Danny dreamed that he and Melinda were together at the family cottage in Wisconsin, swimming in Glimmerglass Lake.

Chapter 10

After sleeping for many hours, Danny and Chip awoke to a soft knocking on the door. Danny looked outside through the window. There was darkness. Then Danny remembered that he was in a place was there was no daytime with warm summer sunshine, but only darkness pierced by artificial light. Danny also felt cold as he pushed off the covers. There was no heat in the room.

"Come in," Danny said. Harold entered, carrying a lantern and pointing it at Danny's face.

"You must arise. Renegade Ralph is ready to meet with you now," Harold said.

"What does he want with us?" Danny said.

"I don't presume to speak for Renegade Ralph," Harold replied.

"Will he help us find my sister Melinda?"

"You will have to ask him directly," Harold said. "Awake your friend."

"Chip, wake up," Danny said, trying to rouse Chip from his sleep. "We have to go."

"Go where?" Chip said. "I'm still tired." Chip then covered his head with the comforter.

"Come on, Chip," Danny said, throwing off the blanket. "We've been summoned by Renegade Ralph. I bet he can help us find Melinda and get out of here."

Chip arose reluctantly, grumbling that he hadn't had anything to eat for breakfast. Then he and Danny put on their shoes and gathered their backpacks to follow Harold through the dark passageways of the house.

Danny looked at his watch. It read four o'clock in the morning. No wonder he was still tired. Obviously, he concluded, people in this world kept very strange hours.

Harold led Danny and Chip to a large set of wooden doors, which creaked when he opened them. Sitting at the far end of the room in an old leather chair whose sides had been ripped open was a man wearing a faded green army uniform that looked like something from World War I. Danny had remembered pictures of similar uniforms in his history books. Danny also noticed that the man was wearing riding boots and had an untrimmed beard that looked like a brown piece of cotton candy had been stuck to his face. Smoke from a cigar circled his head like car exhaust.

"Sir," Harold said respectfully, "The young ones from the topside that we found in the cave."

"Yes," the man said. "Please come in."

"Enter, " Harold said to Danny and Chip. "This is the great Renegade Ralph."

"Come in and sit," Ralph said, gesturing for the boys to take a seat on a small sofa across from him. Danny and Chip walked silently to the sofa and sat down.

"I understand that you've had quite a journey, and that you were almost captured by our enemy," Ralph said.

"Those people—your enemy—took my little sister Melinda. I think they're called the Wanderers," Danny said. "We have to get her back. And we have to get back home to our parents." While he spoke, Danny noticed that Ralph's teeth were brown and that his fingernails were dirty.

"First, let me explain a misconception that you have. Many generations ago, the topsiders—your people—called my ancestors 'wanderers' because we couldn't find steady work and we didn't have a regular home. They were mocked and driven down here. But we no longer use that term of shame. We have homes. We have our mission, just like people in your world. Do not use that name again," Ralph growled.

"Sorry," Danny said sheepishly.

"Now, I understand what you want, but it won't be as easy or as quick to accomplish as you might like," Ralph said. "There are bigger stakes here. Do you know what I mean?"

"I know what the words mean, but I don't know what you mean," Danny said.

"You're a very honest boy," Ralph said, smiling with his stained teeth. "It means that we have been persecuted by our enemy Grandmaster Frank and his lieutenants for generations. And all of us who live beneath the sunlight have been forgotten by the people from your world—the topside. We have been planning an uprising, and the time has almost come to act. I think that you might be able to help us. You will help us, won't you?"

"I don't know," Danny said. "How can we help you? We just want to go home. We won't tell anyone where to find you."

"As if you could," Ralph said. "Could you find your way out of our world?"

Danny and Chip didn't respond. They merely shook their heads.

"I thought not," Ralph said. "So I think that we can help each other. Wouldn't you agree?"

"I guess so," Danny said with some hesitation. "What do you want us to do?"

"We want to rejoin the topside. Your world," Ralph said. "Otherwise we are doomed. We cannot be silent and hide forever. We can no longer live in this world of darkness. We are slowly dying out. We must rejoin your world to survive. I must convince my people that the only hope we have is to leave this place. I want the two of you to help me prepare my people for this journey."

"What do you want us to do?" Danny said.

"You must tell my people about your world and its customs. You must help persuade my people that there is hope in the sunlight, but only doom here in the darkness," Ralph said.

"If we help you, will you help us get my sister back?" Danny said.

"Your sister. Your sister," Ralph yelled. "I am tired of hearing you speak of her! I'll make no promises to you now. I have larger thoughts on my mind. Your sister is just one person. We are talking about an entire people here. Go now until I send further instructions."

Ralph pounded his boot on the floor two times. Harold entered to escort Danny and Chip out of the room.

"What did you do to make him so angry," Harold said.

"I just asked if he would help us find Melinda," Danny said.

"One does not make demands of Ralph. One listens to his wisdom. Do not make the mistake again," Harold said.

Danny and Chip followed Harold through the darkened corridors of the house back to their room. Wooden floorboards creaked as they walked. Lying in his bed, Danny could not sleep. His mind raced. He wondered if Renegade Ralph could be trusted.

Chapter 11

While Danny and Chip were being introduced to Renegade Ralph, Melinda was being transported to the Great Hall that housed the lair of Grandmaster Frank.

After her capture, Melinda's captors lashed her hands and feet with rope and placed a sack over her head. She screamed so loudly that she was gagged with a smelly rag.

She kicked and punched vigorously. She bounced off the sides of the cave's rock walls as she was taken away. She could feel the bruises forming on her arms and legs.

Her captors dropped her to the ground of the muddy cave floor. "Put her to work," she heard someone order. Then she heard an ominous laugh, followed by the sound of footsteps leaving the chamber.

She then felt someone cutting the rope off her arms and taking the wraps off her eyes and mouth. The tingle that she felt told her that blood had began to flow back into her numb hands and feet. But this warm and comforting sensation was interrupted by a frightening sight. She screamed when her eyesight began to adjust to the darkness. Hovering above her were the faces of five boys and girls who stared at her silently with large empty eyes. They carried two lanterns, which lit their faces. She could feel their warm breath upon her skin. She could smell their dirty clothes.

"Get away from me!" she yelled. "You all stink."

The children leapt back but remained in a tight circle around her.

"Stay back," one of them told the others. "You can never tell what a topsider will do. They might eat one of us."

"I'm not going to eat any of you," Melinda said, standing up and wiping the mud off her clothes as best she could. "Don't be ridiculous. What did you call me?"

"A topsider. You come from the world above us," said one little girl with a runny nose.

"My name is Melinda," she said. "Do you know where my brother Danny and his friend Chip are?"

"No, we don't," a boy said who wore a tattered black jacket and old baseball hat. "Maybe they got scared and returned to the topside."

"They wouldn't leave me here," Melinda said. "Even though Danny and I sometimes fight. He is my brother, after all. I'm sure he's terribly worried. Don't you think?"

The children didn't know how to respond to Melinda's comments.

"What's the matter with you all anyway?" Melinda said. "You're just standing there and staring at me. That's awfully rude."

"We were told to watch you," one of the boys said.

"Who told you?" Melinda said.

"Mother Mercedes," the boy said.

"Who's that?" Melinda asked.

"Mother Mercedes takes care of us and gives us jobs to do. We all have very important jobs here in the Great Hall," the boy said.

"Like what?" Melinda said.

"We go on raids to the topside to gather things for the Grandmaster. Like clothes, food, wood, and other bigger stuff. We are in the service of the Grandmaster Frank," the boy said.

"We also dig tunnels and holes," said a girl proudly. The children all nodded in agreement.

"So you're the ones who've been doing all of those things. Destroying houses and stealing things. You've got the adults where I live very confused. And don't you know that stealing is wrong," Melinda said.

"We don't know what you mean. What is this word 'stealing'?" the boy said. "Mother Mercedes called it our duty."

"But what about—" Melinda was interrupted by the sound of heavy footsteps stomping into the small chamber. A large woman entered carrying a lantern in her right hand. Her left hand tightly held the collar of a fur coat to her neck so that the coat would not come undone. She was stooped over and had a green scarf wrapped around her thin red hair. Her face was cut deeply with wrinkles. She wore heavy black boots as if she were preparing to shovel winter snow.

"Get away from her!" the woman barked. All of the children backed away obediently to the sides of the chamber.

"Yes, Mother Mercedes," they all chanted together.

Mother Mercedes walked to Melinda and grabbed her by her shirt, lifting her off the ground so that Melinda was staring right into her inky black eyes.

"Let's get something clear," Mother Mercedes said to Melinda. "Just because you are a topsider doesn't mean anything to me. You are now one of us, and you will work for me. You have no choice."

"I don't have to do anything I don't want to. You're not the boss of me," Melinda said. The children gasped. Not one of them ever had ever challenged Mother Mercedes.

"You little worm!" Mother Mercedes yelled, slamming Melinda up against the wall of the chamber. "You will work and you will follow my orders if you want to live! You are here to work in the service of Grandmaster Frank for the good of the underland."

Mother Mercedes then tossed Melinda back to the ground. "Clara, I hold you responsible for keeping an eye on this one and teaching her our ways."

The girl named Clara came forward and nodded. She had deep blue eyes and short brown hair that sprouted out from her red stocking cap.

"Come, it's time to prepare for our next task. It's time to work. To work!" Mother Mercedes said.

She pushed the children and Melinda out of the chamber and into another dark passage. For the first time, Melinda noticed how cold she was in the dark. She wished that she had brought a jacket.

Chapter 12

Melinda was shivering by the time Mother Mercedes had herded her and the other children to a large room that had many beds lined up against the wall. Each bed had one old sheet and a thin blanket. Only a few beds had pillows.

"You have one hour to eat and rest before I return," Mother Mercedes said, slamming the door behind her.

The children rushed to a steaming black pot that sat in the center of the room. Each of the children dipped a large spoon into the pot and filled their bowls with soup.

Melinda did not join them. Instead, she sat on the end of the bed and watched the others slurp their soup silently.

"You should eat something," Clara said, offering Melinda her bowl.

"It doesn't look very good to me," Melinda said. "My mother could make something better."

Clara shrugged her shoulders, sat next to Melinda, and ate her soup without saying a word. She could see that Melinda was wrapping her arms around herself to keep warm. So she dug under her bed and found a knitted blue wool sweater that she found on one of the raids to the topside. She kept it hidden from the Mother Mercedes as her treasure because it was so beautiful and cozy. She offered the sweater to Melinda.

"Take this," Clara said.

"Thank you," Melinda said. "Why aren't you cold?"

"It's not cold. It's always like this," Clara said.

"It's warm and sunny right now where I live. Flowers are blooming. Everything is bright. Not like here," Melinda said.

"Mother Mercedes better not hear you saying that. She'll punish you," Clara said as she greedily ate her soup.

"Just for saying that I like flowers."

"She will punish you for looking her way when you're not supposed to."

"She sounds like a mean old bitty. Like the old woman who lives next to my parents' house."

"I don't know the word 'bitty,'" Clara said.

"Didn't they teach you anything in school down here?" Melinda responded. "It means an old woman who has a generally mean and unpleasant demeanor."

Clara laughed. "You're funny with your strange words."

"I happen to think my vocabulary is quite good. It's because I read alot. Do you like to read books?"

"We have some old books around here somewhere. I look at the pictures, but I don't understand the words," Clara said.

"I'll teach you, but I don't know how long I'll be here," Melinda said.

"Mother Mercedes forbids us from reading. That is not our duty she says," Clara explained as she slurped the last drops of soup from here bowl.

"Why?" Melinda said.

"Because we must work in the service of the Grandmaster. We don't have time for anything else. And we don't need anything else," Clara said.

"Is that what your Mom and Dad want you to do?" Melinda said.

"I only have one mother, and that's Mother Mercedes. She is the mother of all of us here. She takes care of us. She gives us food and clothes and a place to sleep. Without her, we would have nothing," Clara said.

"But she's ugly and terribly cruel, from what I can tell," Melinda said.

"Be quiet," Clara cautioned. "You can't keep talking like that. If someone hears you, they will tell Mother Mercedes, and I will be punished. No one is to say anything bad against Mother Mercedes. It's a sin."

Melinda looked around the room. Most of the children were busy eating their soup. Some were taking a nap on their beds.

"Sorry," Melinda whispered. "I don't want to get you in trouble."

"Give me back my sweater," Clara said. "I don't want Mother Mercedes to know that I have it. And you have to get used to things around here anyway."

Without the warm of the sweater, Melinda wrapped her arms around her body and shivered as she waited with the others for Mother Mercedes to return.

Chapter 13

Harold deposited Danny and Chip in a room on the top floor of a sagging and damp house down a narrow street from where Renegade Ralph lived. Harold said that it was his house. He lived there alone. Not wanting to be rude, Danny and Chip said it was nice, although they thought otherwise. Harold instructed them to unpack their things and meet him downstairs in ten minutes.

"It's time for you to become worthwhile to us," Harold said, offering the boys cold water and stale cookies.

"What do you mean?" Danny asked.

"For as long as you are here, you need to learn how to survive in this world. You have to become a person of the underland like the rest of us," Harold said. "Renegade Ralph has appointed me as your trainer."

"What are we supposed to do?" Chip asked.

"Today, you will join a team that is scouting the movements of the enemy—the Grandmaster," Harold explained. "Follow me."

Harold led Danny and Chip out of the house and down a dimly lit path through the village to the edge of the dark lake. Danny and Chip did not have their flashlights with them. Harold did not carry a lantern. So they stumbled often on the slippery rock beneath their feet. It was hard for them to see the contours in the rocky path. But Harold didn't have a problem. He moved as swiftly and confidently over the rocks as a cat or any other creature accustomed to almost total darkness.

A group of eight other boys was awaiting Harold, Danny, and Chip as they approached the lake's edge. Danny noticed that the boys ranged in age from about five or six years old to eleven or twelve years. They were dressed like the others he had met so far in the underland—in a motley combination of old and dirty clothes that were layered together to create warmth. One boy wore a tattered sweatshirt over a jacket, while another boy had wrapped a wool scarf around his head as a substitute for a stocking cap.

As they approached, Danny smelled a stench coming from the boys. But Danny thought to himself that he had not bathed in a few days either, so he would soon have the same aroma that they now had. He wasn't looking forward to becoming smelly because he enjoyed being clean. He surveyed his clothes. He could see that they were smeared with dried mud from crawling through the cave passageways. He frowned and sighed when he saw how messy he looked. Chip, on the other hand, could care less that his clothes were dirty.

The group of boys all nodded in silent recognition as Harold walked up to them. It was obvious to Danny and Chip that Harold commanded great respect, or fear, among the boys.

"You have probably all heard the rumors that two from the topside have joined our community," Harold said. "Well, here they are. That one is called Danny and the other is called Chip. Ralph has instructed me to teach them the ways of the underland. And in turn they will teach us about the topside. This is their first mission. You are to help them as much as you would help me. Do you understand?"

The boys all nodded and mumbled "Yes." Danny could see that they all were eyeing him and Chip suspiciously.

"Good," Harold said. "Now let's go. We have to be back in two hours."

"Harold," Danny said. "What about flashlights or lamps so that we can see. Chip and I left ours back in the room."

"That is the lesson you will learn today—how to move around without light but by feel and a sense of place," Harold said. "Just follow us and hold on to one of the boys in front of you."

Harold led the group up a perilously inclined path from the lake to a small opening in the grand cavern's wall. The group squeezed through an opening that seemed to Danny and Chip no larger than a basketball. Danny and Chip were in the middle of the pack of boys that snaked through the darkness. Danny was glad he could reach out and feel the clothes of the boy in front of him. The boy's presence comforted Danny, but the smell in tight quarters did not, however.

Occasionally, Harold would instruct Danny and Chip to concentrate on how far they thought they were going and in what direction. "Keep track of how many steps you have taken and whether you were going up, down, or sideways. If you know your sense of place, you do not need light," Harold said.

Danny counted his steps and made a mental note of the direction he was heading. When he started concentrating like this, the cave seemed a less scary place.

Just as Danny's comfort level was rising, Harold told the group to stop and gather around him and stay quiet. Danny and Chip crawled to a small, narrow slit in the rock through which a pale light flowed. "There is the enemy," Harold whispered.

It took a few seconds for Danny and Chip's eyes to adjust the faint light. But when they could focus they saw a grand cavern filled with large houses that surrounded a town square. An underground river flowed through the village, across which were arched wooden bridges like Danny had seen in photos of Japan. They could see troops marching in the square.

"The Grandmaster is preparing his Brotherhood of Knights for battle," Harold said. "This is what we have feared."

To the left of the square, Danny saw another group of people marching in single file behind a large woman. They were heading to a ladder that ascended to an opening in the wall of the cavern. On closer inspection, Danny could see that they were small children.

"Chip, look over there," Danny said, pointing to the children climbing the ladder.

"Danny!" Chip said. "I think I see Melinda. There, in the red shirt and blue jeans! She's OK."

Danny looked closer and did see Melinda. "Harold. Harold. I see my sister. We have to go down," Danny said, looking for a way to slip through the opening.

Harold grabbed him forcefully and pushed him against the wall. "We're not going to do anything of the sort. Not now. It's too dangerous. We will all be captured. And then how will you return to your world, if that is what you wish to do? You have to learn to think. You have to learn to act when the time is right."

Harold motioned for the group to return. Danny dutifully followed. There was nothing he could do now. But at least he knew where he could find Melinda when the time was right.

Chapter 14

On the way back through the snaking passages, Danny couldn't take his mind off the sight of his sister climbing the ladder. He was so close to her, but he could do nothing.

He was coming to the conclusion that neither Harold nor Renegade Ralph was going to let him and Chip return to their homes, in spite of what they were told. They might be prisoners in the underland forever. For the first time since arriving, Danny felt scared and desperate. He loved to dream of far away places, but the underworld was not what he had in mind.

He looked at the motley group of boys who were under Harold's command. Their clothes were old and dirty, and the food that they ate everyday was boring and bad. Didn't they ever have a desire to escape themselves, and go live where he and Chip lived? They must know routes out of here, but yet they chose to remain. Danny was perplexed.

Danny, Chip, Harold, and the boys scrambled down from a small passage to the narrow path that went past the dark lake in the cavern. The water was calm and looked like a mirror. But the silence and tranquillity were shattered when a large black creature thrust through the surface and grabbed one of the boys at the front of the line in his jaws that dripped with water. To Danny, it looked like a giant black snake or worm. It had no eyes, only a large head with fierce teeth. This must be the demon of the lake that Harold mentioned when he first brought them here, Danny thought.

Neither Danny nor the other boys had time to scream. One second the boy called Luke was walking, and the next second he was pulled below the surface of the lake by the creature and was gone. The boys were too stunned to scream or cry.

Harold yelled at the boys to flee as fast as they could to the houses on the other side of the lake and to stay as far from the shore of the lake as possible. The boys struggled over the slippery rocks. Some of them tripped and cut and bruised themselves. They all returned to the village gasping for air but safe.

The villagers came out of their homes to greet the returning boys. Harold explained what happened. Danny noticed that no one shed a tear. They all nodded their heads quietly while Harold said that Luke was an excellent boy and would be missed. "We must have done something to anger the demon," Harold said. "We all have to be more cautious."

"But there is more dire news," Harold continued. "We discovered that the Grandmaster's knights are preparing for battle. I have to make a report to Renegade Ralph and seek his counsel."

Harold departed for Ralph's house, leaving Danny and Chip with the boys in the village square.

Sam walked up to Danny and pushed him to the ground. "You and your friend caused Luke's death. You are a curse on our village. You angered the demon. You'll never return to the land of light now," Sam said, gesturing for the other boys to follow him.

Chip helped Danny up off the ground. Danny could see the fear in Chip's eyes. They had to figure out a way to escape the underland.

Chapter 15

According to Danny's watch, an entire day had passed since Harold went to see Renegade Ralph. It had been three days since they had stumbled onto the underland. But time in the underland was different. Sometimes Danny and Chip would fall asleep and it would be the middle of the afternoon in their world. At other times, they would be wide awake at two o'clock in the morning. No sunlight came through their windows announcing a new day. No stars filled the sky at night. No wind rustled the window curtains. Only darkness and silence, broken only by the occasional sound of water dripping from the cavern walls.

The food Danny and Chip had brought with them was gone. They were forced to eat the food that was scavenged by the villagers from the topside. Danny and Chip realized that they were eating their neighbors' garbage. Sometimes they would gag on what they were given to eat. But they had no choice. After a while, any food was good food. The rhythm of the village revolved around expeditions to get food and other supplies to sustain the villagers. That was the only job that people had.

Danny and Chip soon became bored with life in the village. So they began looking around for something interesting to do. They stumbled upon a large building that looked like a warehouse. With their flashlights in hand, they entered the building. It was filled to the ceiling with all junk that had been stolen from the topside. Piles of old clothes were stashed in one corner. Old furniture was stored in another corner. Tables, chairs, and sofas of various sizes and styles littered the room.

"Look," Chip said. "I see some baseball bats and gloves."

Danny and Chip rushed to the pile, pulling our several wood and aluminum bats and some infield and outfield gloves, even a catcher's mitt.

"Now all we need is a ball," Danny said. "There must be one here somewhere."

They dived into the junk pile again. Chip eventually found a baseball that was covered in grass stains, but otherwise it was good.

They carried the equipment to the village square, which had the most lights hanging from wooden poles. The lighting was poor, but still bright enough to play catch and hit the ball.

Danny loved the sound of the ball hitting a leather glove. He and Chip tossed the ball joyfully across the square. Soon, Sam and other underland children began to gather and watch silently.

Danny stopped tossing the ball and addressed Sam: "Do you want to learn how to play?"

"Play what?" Sam said.

"Baseball of course. This is what Chip and I are playing," Danny said.

"Why should we?" Sam said. Sam and the others were still angry with Danny and Chip, whom they believed were a curse that caused the death of their friend.

"Because it's fun," Chip said.

"Come on," Danny said. "Renegade Ralph instructed us to teach you about our world. This game is an important part of our world."

"Very important," Chip said.

When Sam and the others heard the name of Renegade Ralph invoked, they decided that it would be wise to listen to the strange boys from the topside.

"OK. Please teach us this game of . . ." Sam said reluctantly.

"Baseball," Chip said.

Chip and Danny showed he children where the bases should

go. They improvised, using old grain sacked for the bases. Then they passed out as many gloves as they could find. Danny pitched for one side and Chip for the other. Because they had never played baseball before, the underland children swung awkwardly at the ball. They also couldn't catch it very well.

But Danny and Chip patiently showed the children the fine points of fielding and hitting. Because the game was played on rock, Danny and Chip decided that sliding would not be a good idea.

Soon, the children caught on, sending balls flying to the outfield and bouncing onto the rocks beyond. Laughter and cheers echoed in the cavern, along with the crack of the bats and the pounding of leather. Adults came out of their houses to see what was happening. At first they were confused, but they soon caught on to the game's rules and starting cheering when one side or the other made a hit or caught a flyball in the dim light.

Danny and Chip enjoyed the competition. They had never played a night game in Rivertown. But in the underland, all games would be night games.

The game was closely contested. By hitting a home run that nearly hit the top of the cavern's ceiling in the last inning, Chip ensured that his team won the game. For some reason, however, when Danny and Chip said that the game was over, the children all walked away silently with the adults of the village, leaving Chip and Danny alone in the village square, surrounded by discarded gloves and bats. Chip and Danny always thought that one of the best parts of playing baseball was recounting the action after a game. But not here. Not in the underland. The children didn't even say thanks for being taught how to play baseball.

Danny and Chip decided that the children of underland had a lot to learn before being ready to journey to the topside.

Chapter 16

Melinda soon became bored sitting all day in the smelly and stuffy dormitory with the other children, waiting for orders from Mother Mercedes. She was used to playing outside with her friends or sitting on her comfortable bed and reading book after book.

She asked Clara to show her where the books were. Clara took her to an old oak trunk. Clara lifted the creaky lid. In the trunks were hundreds of books that had been taken from homes on the topside. Melinda began to dig through the pile with delight. Finding the books was like finding fresh air.

Melinda found one her favorite books: *Alice's Adventures in Wonderland*. She began reading silently in the corner, as the other children slept or talked quietly. For the first time since she had arrived in the underland, Melinda had forgotten about the cold and the damp and how much she wanted to return home. She remembered when he mother had first read this book to her before she went to bed. When she was younger, Melinda longed for the day when she could read for herself. It was like magic when the odd black and white symbols on a white page suddenly meant something that she could understand.

After about thirty minutes of reading quietly, Melinda arose and sat on the end of Clara's bed in the center of the room. None of the other children took much notice of her.

Then Melinda started reading aloud from the first chapter. She read about Alice, the White Rabbit, and the rabbit hole.

Clara and the other children immediately look around for Mother Mercedes, who would surely punish Melinda for reading and punish the others for listening.

"Please stop," Clara said. "Mother Mercedes forbids reading."

"She's not here," Melinda said, pausing briefly from reading. "This is a terrific story. You'll love it. Someone keep watch for the old bitty and I will continue."

A boy named Freddy volunteered to stay by the door and watch for Mother Mercedes. The children then gathered around Melinda as she continued the story of Alice's fall down the rabbit hole. The craned their necks forward to hear every word Melinda spoke. They had never heard a tale as extraordinary as that of Alice.

Soon, the children began interrupting Melinda with questions. "Where does Alice live? Can rabbits and mice really talk?"

Melinda gladly answered the questions that were tossed her way. The reading session came to an abrupt halt, however, when Freddy signaled that Mother Mercedes was approaching. All the children scurried back to their beds. Melinda returned the book to the oak trunk and pretended she was asleep.

Mother Mercedes pushed the door open furiously. She surveyed the room with her cold eyes. "Something's been going on here," she said. "I can smell it. Whatever it is you're hiding, I will find it. Whatever it is you're thinking, I will discover it. Don't think you little vermin can outsmart me!"

As Melinda lay in the corner, she thought to herself: "We'll see about that."

Chapter 17

Danny and Chip organized several other baseball games under the dim lights in the village square. The children played the games enthusiastically and with increasing skill. The games made Danny and Chip forget their predicament, at least for a little while. But no matter how hard they tried, they could not really make friends with the other children in the underland. It seemed as if the children were programmed to act in a certain way. They weren't as free and spontaneous as were Danny and Chip. After each game, they just left Danny and Chip alone to pass the hours. How could they teach the children of the underland about their world if no one would talk to them to listen to them. As each day passed, Danny and Chip felt more isolated.

Left alone one day in the village square, Danny and Chip sat down on small pile of rocks to contemplate what they would do next. They had been in the underland for two weeks, but it had seemed much longer since they had felt that warmth of the sun and the feel of a summer's breeze on their skins.

"Danny," Chip said. "Do you think that we could find our way out of here on our own?"

"I don't know, Chip," Danny said. "I think I could find my way back to the Grandmaster's cavern. I was paying attention to where we were going before. I think I've memorized the path in my head. But from there I wouldn't know where to go."

"But remember when we saw Melinda on the ladder," Chip said. "I bet that ladder goes to the topside."

"Yeah, that's right," Danny responded. "But what would happen to us if we were captured by the Grandmaster's knights?"

"It couldn't be any worse than being kept here or being eaten by that thing in the lake," Chip said.

"But Renegade Ralph promised to help us if we helped him," Danny said.

"How can we teach when everyone ignores us?" Chip said. "I'm sure Renegade Ralph will get mad at us for not keeping our end of the bargain."

"But it's not our fault," Danny said.

"Do you think that matters to Ralph?" Chip said.

"I guess not. But if we tried to escape we could get lost again or be captured, or worse," Danny said.

"I don't care. We can't stay here. We don't belong here," Chip said.

"Then let's try to leave later today, when everyone is asleep," Danny said.

"Quiet," Chip said. "The villagers are coming."

The villagers gathered in the square, silently staring at Danny and Chip.

In the distance, they could see Renegade Ralph walking towards the gathered crowd. A villager motioned to Danny and Chip to leave the pile of rocks on which they were sitting and make way for Ralph.

Ralph climbed upon the rocks to address the villagers.

"I know that you have been waiting for me to comment on the death of young Luke. He shouldn't have died so young. But sometimes young soldiers have to die for a greater good. Luke was one of those young soldiers," Ralph said.

"But he will not have died in vain if we can finally rid ourselves of the demon in the lake. We must do this quickly before anyone else is lost. For we need all of our resources to prepare for the impending attack of the Grandmaster's knights. The time is at hand when the Grandmaster seeks to rid our world of his competitors. Our defeat would mean a defeat of all the generations before us who fought against servitude to the Grandmaster or humiliation from the people who live in the world of light. We cannot let this happen. We will not let this happen!"

The villagers roared and cheered their approval at Renegade Ralph's words.

"Young ones," he said, addressing Danny and Chip. "You must kill the demon of the lake before we will help you out of the underland. If you do not rid us of the demon, you will never see your world again. You have forty-eight hours to bring us the carcass of demon!"

"The demon! The demon! The demon!" The villagers chanted as they danced in a circle around Danny and Chip.

Danny and Chip rushed to Harold looking for an explanation of Ralph's unexpected condition.

"Harold, how can we kill the demon when no one else has been able to?" Danny said. "That wasn't part of the deal. We were just supposed to teach your people about our world. We've been trying."

"But people just ignore us," Chip said.

"I cannot do anything for you," Harold said. "Ralph's word is law. I'm sorry. The rules have changed. Now go, you must prepare yourself for your task."

Harold walked away with his head down. In his heart, he wished that Danny and Chip had never discovered his world. They were not prepared for its harshness and cold brutality.

Chapter 18

Harold returned an hour later to find Danny and Chip still sitting quietly in the village square. They had been discussing how they might kill the demon when nobody else could. They hadn't yet thought of any brilliant ideas.

"Follow me," he said.

Harold led them from the village square to a large storage shed on the edge of the village. The old wooden door creaked open. Using an old lamp for light, Harold showed Danny and Chip a vast assortment of ropes, knifes, pitchforks, poles, and many other unrecognizable instruments.

"This is what we can give you to fight the demon," Harold said. "Take anything that you want."

"How do you expect us to kill the demon when you haven't been able to?" Danny asked.

"It is a daunting task, I admit," Harold said. "But Ralph has spoken. You must try. I did not wish for this burden to fall upon you. But it has, and you must deal with it as best that you can." Harold left the lamp with the boys and departed the shed.

"What do you think we should use?" Chip asked.

"Let's take a closer look at this stuff," Danny said. "I think that rope would be good. And something long and sharp to stick the creature with—like these pitchforks."

"And how about something heavy, like these iron poles," Chip said.

"That's good," Danny said. After gathering their tools of combat, Danny and Chip planned their strategy.

"The demon jumped out of the water with no warning," Danny said. "We need to coax it out of the water."

"How about a decoy?" Chip said. "Let's ask Harold for some old clothes. We can stuff it with straw or old newspaper or something. And then set the decoy along the side of the lake."

"That's a good idea," Danny said. "Let's go."

The fear and dread Danny and Chip felt had suddenly given way to enthusiasm. They found Harold, who helped them find old clothes and a stash of yellow newspapers that were over fifty years old. Danny and Chip fashioned something that looked like a scarecrow. They were ready to battle the lake demon.

They dragged their decoy and weapons along the edge of the dark lake. After placing the decoy near the water's edge, Danny and Chip took cover behind a large pile of stones, and waited. They waited for several hours and nothing happened.

And then they saw a dark form begin to surface. It was the lake demon. It raised its eyeless head out of the water, and seemed to sniff the air. Then it glided to the edge of the lake, getting closer to the decoy. Danny and Chip grabbed their ropes and pitchforks tightly. This might be their chance they thought

Then Danny and Chip saw another creature arise from the dark water. And then another. Until there was six of the creatures, some large and some small. They all gathered by the edge of the lake. And then the largest creature spoke.

"It really was a very good idea. The stupid old villagers never would have thought of it. We applaud you," the creature said in perfect English.

Danny and Chip looked at each other in amazement. They couldn't believe what they were hearing.

"I know you must think there you're imagining things. But, yes, we can talk your language. And pretty well I might add," the creature said. "Come out. We won't hurt you."

"But you killed that boy named Luke, and many others the

villagers tell us," Danny yelled from behind the rock, not wanting to show himself.

"Yes. All that is true. We have been waging a battle against the villagers. But we were here first, living peacefully for thousands of years since the time of the great icebergs. Then the humans came along about a century ago and tried to destroy us. We've just been fighting back, although we are passive creatures by nature," the lake demon said. "But when you are threatened, you have to protect yourself. We would have liked to make friends with the humans, but they began attacking us from the start."

"You must know that we were sent here to kill you," Danny said, peering over the rock to see the creature.

"But you were sent here reluctantly. We can hear conversations hundreds of feet away. Our hearing is very keen. We know that you mean us no harm," the creature said. "Come out from your hiding place, please. Trust us."

Danny and Chip slowly crept out from behind the rock, still clutching their weapons just in case of a surprise attack by the creatures. They slowly walked to the shore.

"There. You see. We don't want to harm you," the leader of the creatures said.

"But will you stop terrorizing the villagers?" Danny asked.

The creatures all joined together to whisper among themselves in a language that Danny couldn't understand.

"If the villagers agree to leave us alone. We will leave them alone. This battle has gone on much too long," the creature said.

"Then follow us back to the village and we will tell everyone the news," Danny said.

As Danny and Chip walked along the path back to the village, the creatures glided next to them in the water.

"You better stay under water until I explain to the villagers what's happening," Danny instructed the creatures.

Danny and Chip reentered the village and stopped at the village square. They stood on the very rock where Renegade Ralph had spoken. They yelled as loud as they could that they had conquered the lake demon. The villagers gathered, including Renegade Ralph.

Ralph spoke: "What are you yelling about? I see no dead demon. Where is the proof of your conquest?"

"We didn't need to kill the demon. But we have saved your village anyway," Danny said, who then turned toward the lake and said: "You can come up now."

The villagers gasped in fear as the six creatures rose slowly from the lake. All that could be heard was water dripping from their heads back into the lake.

"Don't be afraid," said Danny. "The creatures do not want to harm you any longer. Listen for yourselves."

"The young boy is right," the leader of the creatures said. "We want to end the feud with you. Stop trying to kill us, and we will end our retaliations against you."

"Is this a trick?" Ralph said. "Some kind of witchcraft?"

"It's no trick," Danny said. "Do you agree with the terms?"

"If it means that there will be no more bloodshed, then I accept," Ralph said.

The creatures all nodded and then slowly sunk back down into the lake. All were hidden except the leader, who spoke: "You owe your lives to these young boys. They should be praised. Young ones, we will be there for you if you need us. I am Arturis. I have spoken." And then Arturis disappeared beneath the lake waters.

"Danny and Chip, you have done well," Harold said. "Three cheers for the boys!"

The villagers cheered and gathered around Danny and Chip to thank and praise them.

Later that night in their room, Danny and Chip reveled in their good fortune. They believed that surely now Renegade Ralph will grant them their freedom.

Chapter 19

Melinda continued to read to the other children about Alice when Mother Mercedes wasn't around. It kept her mind from the fact that she was a prisoner deep underground, far away from her home on the topside.

Even though she had never been caught reading, she could feel Mother Mercedes' black eyes staring at her, boring into her like a worm into an apple.

One day as Melinda and the children slept, they were awakened by the slam of the door and a screeching yell. "Get up, you good for nothing dirty vermin! You have a job to do!" Mother Mercedes barked as she walked down the length of the room hitting the groggy children on their feet with a long wooden stick.

Mother Mercedes led Melinda and the other children up wooden ladders to steep passageways in the cave. Melinda didn't know if there would be sunlight or darkness when they reached the top. She has lost track of time and days of the week.

After nearly an hour of hard climbing, Mother Mercedes called for the group to stop. She went forward and addressed the children in a small cavern that looked liked it had been carved out with tools.

"The Grandmaster's guardians have been here before us to prepare the site. They have destroyed another of the topsiders' houses so that we may live. Long live the Guardians!" she yelled.

"Long live the guardians!" the children replied.

"You know what you need to do," Mother Mercedes continued.

"Bring back everything that you can for the good of your fellow villagers. And remain as silent as cats."

Mother Mercedes then walked directly to Melinda and said: "Don't think that you'll get away. You're one of us now. If you try to run, I will catch you. And I will punish you. You will do as the others. You will work."

Melinda started shaking, but remained silent.

Mother Mercedes then rolled aside a stone that uncovered another passage that led to a crater. Fresh air streamed in from above; the first fresh air that Melinda had breathed into her lungs for weeks. Emerging into the crater, Melinda looked at the night sky. It was warm and cloudy, and the ground was wet and muddy. It must have rained recently, she thought. An orange moon hung in the sky, looking like a ripe orange.

In the darkness, she could see the remains of a house in the crater. There was broken furniture and piles of shattered wood. Clothes were scattered in the rubble, covered with dirt and plaster dust. She now knew who was destroying the houses in Rivertown, but she couldn't tell anyone. She couldn't scream or run away. She took Mother Mercedes' threat seriously.

She was ordered to carry as much as she could down the steep passage cut into the side of the cavern. Load after load of clothes, wood, furniture, roof shingles, and other remnants of the house were lowered down the passage. Those things that didn't fit were left behind. The children worked quickly and silently. Many children, including Melinda, cut their hands on sharp pieces of wood or nails, but no one yelled or cried. They were disciplined and efficient scavengers.

Surveying it all with a scowl was Mother Mercedes. When she determined that the children had taken enough of the valuable materials, she ordered them to return to the small cavern, which was now brimming with all of the things that the children had pilfered from above. Melinda and the children sat down, breathing heavily from their exertion.

"Good work," Mother Mercedes said. "Grandmaster Frank will

be pleased. But your work is not over, for we must take our prizes back to the village so that the guardians can destroy all signs that we were ever here. Get up. Carry everything that you can. We must return at once."

Each child helped the other strap as much as possible onto another's back. Clara tied a pile of clothes and a heavy mirror onto Melinda's back—just big enough so that Melinda could make it through the passages back to the village.

On Mother Mercedes' order, the children began the long and painful march back through the damp, dark passages. They were all sweating from the weight of their heavy loads. When one of the children faltered, Mother Mercedes kicked them with her thick black boot. All Melinda could think about was a bowl of hot soup and lying down on her bed.

She looked up once and saw the eyes of Mother Mercedes riveted on her. "You will never leave. Your body and soul are mine forever," Mother Mercedes said. She began laughing and then coughing uncontrollably. She spit once on the floor and then moved to the front of the line.

Chapter 20

Mother Mercedes led the children back to the village in a grand procession of plunder. Weighed down by stacks of dirty clothes, broken furniture, and scraps of wood, Mother Mercedes maneuvered the tired children into a large plaza that was brightly lit.

Grandmaster Frank's followers stopped their chores and began to gather in the plaza. Then the Grandmaster's burly guardians arrived, pushing their way to the front of the awaiting crowd. Mother Mercedes barked at the children to place their things at the foot of a large stage erected in the center of the plaza.

Melinda joyously unloaded the stack of clothes and the mirror that she had been carrying for hours. Her whole body had begun to cramp because of carrying so much weight while stooped over in small passages. She wanted to lie on the ground, but she knew that she could not. Mother Mercedes was watching her like a vulture.

As the children unloaded their packs of stolen goods, a huge mountain of used and broken items began growing in front of the stage. The villagers and the guardians began applauding as the stack grew higher. To them, the dirty, broken, and dusty pile was like a mountain of gold.

When the last child had placed his pack on the ground, a bugle sounded. The guardians snapped to order and began to form an aisle to the stage through the gathered crowd.

"What's happening?" Melinda asked Clara.

"Quiet. Lower your head. Grandmaster Frank is coming," Clara said.

Melinda kept her head bowed but still managed to glimpse Grandmaster Frank as he walked past her to the stage. He was tall, with a barrel chest and a huge head that was covered with long, flowing red hair, like the mane of a lion. His nose was sharp, like a hatchet. He wore gold and silver rings on each finger and a diamond earring in his right ear. His long black coat had a fur collar and made a swishing sound as he walked. His black boots were brightly polished and reflected the lights that were illuminating the plaza.

Grandmaster Frank climbed to the stage and stretched out his arms, as if he were embracing everyone whom was present.

"Let us give praise to Mother Mercedes and her band of providers. She has once again done us all a great service," he said.

"All praise Mother Mercedes!" the villagers chanted. Mother Mercedes humbly bowed to the crowd.

"People of the underland," Grandmaster Frank continued. "Two great battles draw nearer. We must all be prepared for them. In the first, we will destroy Renegade Ralph and all those who follow him. He is a heretic. He must be destroyed."

"The second battle will be more difficult but more momentous. We will wage battle directly against the topsiders themselves—face to face, no longer sneaking through the shadows like we didn't exist. We do exist. We do breathe the same air as the topsiders. We have the same dreams, the dreams of our ancestors that were banished so long ago."

"And we will not fight with spears and sticks. We will fight with the ultimate weapon, and we will prevail!" Grandmaster Frank screamed.

As he finished his proclamation, a group of guardians pulled to the stage a wagon covered with a tarp. They threw off the tarp. Loaded onto the wagon were hundreds of guns and rifles that the guardians have been hoarding for years.

Grandmaster Frank motioned to one guardian, who tossed him a rifle. Grandmaster Frank raised the weapon above his head. "Look closely. These are the tools of freedom, the instruments of liberation. Our voices will boom with the sounds of a thousand bursts of fire!"

The villagers cheered and stomped their feet on the ground.

"We shall see the sunlight!" Grandmaster Frank said.

"We shall see the sunlight! We shall see the sunlight!" the villagers replied.

Grandmaster Frank stepped down from the stage and walked through the crowd. The villagers each tried to touch his hand or his long dark coat. Melinda was pushed aside and nearly trampled by people trying to get closer to Grandmaster Frank. She began crawling on the ground to get away from the crush of people. She watched from a distance as the villagers of underland followed Grandmaster Frank through the village to his palace high in the wall of the cavern.

Chapter 21

Since arriving in the underland over a month ago, Danny slept fitfully, waking every few hours from bad dreams. He often dreamed of being pursued by a giant with no face. He jumped out of bed. The room was pitch black and silent except for his own heavy breathing. There was no breeze through the trees, no sounds of crickets or birds or distant trains. There was no clock ticking or water dripping.

Danny awoke to find Chip sleeping serenely in the bed next to his. Danny wished that he could sleep as soundly as Chip. Since they had rid the village of the danger of the lake creatures, Harold had given them extra food. For the first time since their arrival, Danny and Chip felt healthy. They were less fearful of being killed. But Danny still agonized about how he would find Melinda and return to his home and his parents.

Did his parents think he was kidnapped or murdered? Were the people of Rivertown looking for them? Would they think to look in the quarry caves?

Danny's mind swirled like a carnival ride when he heard a sound outside of the window. He grabbed his flashlight and pointed it at the narrow alley between the buildings. The beam of light startled three men wearing black clothes and miner's hats.

Then there was a shot and the sound of broken glass above Danny's head. Danny ducked down just before another shot exploded through the window and wedged in the wall. Danny crawled over to Chip's bed and pulled him to the floor.

"What's going on?" Chip asked, still half asleep.

"Someone is shooting at us." Danny said. "Stay down. I'll go get Harold."

Danny carefully crawled to the door and then into the hall. Harold was already there, carrying an old sword that looked like it was last used in the Civil War.

"Harold!" Danny cried. "There are three men in the alley carrying guns. I surprised them with my flashlight and they started shooting."

"Stay here," Harold said. "I'll go get Ralph's guards."

The entire village had been awakened by the gun shots. People came streaming out of their houses. An old man and his wife stood on their porch to survey the commotion. Another shot cut through the darkness and struck the old man, who slumped to the ground. His wife screamed and pointed to a pile of rocks near the dark lake's edge.

Harold and other men from the village quickly began running to where the woman pointed. More shots were fired at them. They took cover. Their only weapons were sticks and antique swords that were beginning to rust.

The gunfire then stopped as quickly as it had begun. Silence once again cloaked Renegade Ralph's village. The villagers gathered around the fallen body of the old man named Holmes as Harold and the others returned. They all comforted Holmes' wife May. No one could remember anyone in the village ever having been killed by a gun. The horror of Holmes' death stunned everyone.

The mumbles and soft cries were interrupted by the excited sounds of a boy named Jake, who came running from around the corner, panting.

"Quick!" he said. "Come with me!"

Harold led the villagers into the alley that ran beneath Danny's window. Scrawled on the wall in red paint was this ominous warning: "The one ruler is the Grandmaster. Honor him or perish."

Chapter 22

Holmes was dressed in the best clothes that he had, but even these garments were old and ragged, consisting of various pieces of fabric sown together by his now widowed wife.

Holmes was placed on a wooden sled and carried by a group of men from the village to a cave carved deep into the rock on a ledge above the village. The entire village followed behind their fallen neighbor in a silent procession of respect that was led by Renegade Ralph, who wore a black bandana. Everyone carried candles to light their way.

No one cried. No one spoke as the villagers reached the ledge. Holmes' body was placed deep into the cave by the same men who had carried him. They then covered the entrance to the cave with heavy stones. It was then that Renegade Ralph spoke:

"We share May's love of her beloved Holmes. He was an important member of our community for nearly eighty years. His father was among the first group of our ancestors to be banished to the underland by the topsiders. As such, he is a direct link to our proud yet sad heritage. He will be missed. But we will survive as one. For now, we face an enemy just like us. An enemy of our fellow underlanders who have spurned us and attacked us. They seek to degrade us just as the topsiders have done for decades. But we have pride. We are not the slaves of the Grandmaster. Let us prepare to defend ourselves. We will fight with the image of our slain friend Holmes burned into our minds."

The villagers then turned to follow Renegade Ralph back down to the village. Danny thought that the line of people with their lanterns looked like a glowing snake in the total darkness of the underland. Danny and Chip shared the feeling of sadness displayed by the villagers with whom they had been living for over a month. Neither one had ever seen anyone killed, or even dead. Both of their grandfathers had died before they were born, and their grandmothers were still alive.

But their thoughts of mourning quickly turned to concern, for Chip and Danny were now caught in the middle of a civil war between two groups of people that no one from his world even knew existed. Life and death decisions were being made deep in the earth as his friends and neighbors went about their business in the sunshine.

Danny's thoughts then turned again to Melinda, who was living with people who were now labeled the enemy. As he headed back to the village, Danny wondered what Harold or Renegade Ralph had in store for him and Chip now.

Chapter 23

After the funeral procession for Holmes, the villagers became more quiet and sullen than they usually were. Danny and Chip would bring out the balls, bats, and gloves. But no one wanted to play baseball.

They spent most of their time in their room or by the rocky shore of the dark lake playing catch. Danny and Chip were becoming bored. There were no fields or parks in which to play, no television to watch, no music to enjoy. Danny was able to find some old *National Geographic* magazines to read and pass the time, while Chip just began sleeping more and more, sometimes fourteen to sixteen hours a day.

As Danny looked at pictures of exotic places like the Amazon jungles or the wilds of Borneo, he wondered what the people of the underland would think of these places. To them, they would seem like planets in a distant solar system, if they even knew or cared about planets or stars.

Danny was dreaming of climbing in the Andes mountains, while Chip snoozed beside him as Harold approached the day after Holmes' burial.

"Danny. Chip," Harold said. "I have some important news from Ralph."

"Chip, wake up," Danny said, poking his friend in the forehead with his finger.

"Is it time for school?" Chip said groggily, while rolling over on his side. "I feel sick today."

"Chip, wake up!" Danny yelled.

"What? OK. OK. Stop yelling," Chip said, rubbing his eyes and pushing his baseball cap back on this head.

"Ralph has made an important decision that will affect all of us," Harold said. "We are going to strike Grandmaster Frank before he can overwhelm us."

"A surprise attack?" Danny asked.

"Yes," Harold said. "Everyone has been asked to gather any type of weapons they can find for the great battle."

"What about us?" Danny asked.

"Ralph has a new proposition for you. If you fight with us and help us to victory, you will be allowed to return to your world."

"But we could be killed," Chip said.

"Ralph keeps changing the rules. First it's one thing and then another, and we are still here," Danny reminded Harold.

"We have treated you well even though you are not one of us. You shouldn't be complaining," Harold scolded them.

"I thought you were our friend. I thought you understood us," Danny said.

"I don't want harm to come to you, but I am not your friend. I cannot be. Enough of this nonsense. You must be prepared to fight. It's your only choice," Harold said.

"No one here keeps their word," Danny said. "We're not soldiers. We're just kids. We can't kill."

"We just want to get out of here," Chip said.

"Look at your choices. If you don't fight with us, you might be killed or enslaved by the Grandmaster's guardians. At least in fighting with us, you will be in charge of your own destiny. I know these are difficult choices because you are just boys. But life is different here. You need to decide within twelve hours, for that is when Ralph has decided that we will begin the battle for liberation."

After Harold departed, Danny and Chip sat silently. They were faced with choices that they never had imagined in Rivertown.

As they wondered about their fate, Arturis rose from the depths of the lake.

"What has been going on?" he asked. "The commotion has been disturbing us."

Danny and Chip told Arturis of the sneak attack, the murder of Holmes, and the battle plans of Renegade Ralph.

"They will not learn," Arturis said. "But I will keep my promise. You need not be afraid." And then Arturis departed.

Danny and Chip walked back to the village to find the villagers gathering rusty rakes, shovels, iron poles—anything that could be remotely considered a weapon.

Chapter 24

Renegade Ralph's rag-tag band of warriors assembled in the village square for final instructions from their leader. Ralph appeared carrying a long sword that, even polished, still showed signs of rust. He wore an old leather football jersey on which was painted a "V." Danny wondered what the letter signified.

"The hour has come," Ralph said solemnly from atop a wooden crate. "The hour has come when we will take our future into our own hands. When we will seek to vanquish our tormentors and enemies and regain our stature and dignity. I regret that it has come to this. But if we are smart, and take the enemy by surprise, we will be victorious!"

He raised his sword high above his head, and the villagers all cried "Victory!" Danny and Chip joined them, for if not in their hearts at least in their minds, they were now allies of the villagers. These poor and forgotten people gave them food and shelter. They were the only family the two boys had known for forty days. But neither boy really wanted to fight. They were playing along so they wouldn't make Harold or Ralph suspicious about their true desires to escape when they had the chance.

Danny and Chip each carried heavy baseball bats that they had used during their games in the village square. They weren't sure how effective the bats would be as weapons, but they both enjoyed the feel of the bats in their hands. They longed for the day when they could play on the green grass in the warm summer sun.

Ralph, with his lieutenant Harold at his side, motioned for the villagers to follow them up a steep path to an opening high in the cavern. All able-bodied villagers were making the march. Only young children and the elders who were too weak to make the arduous climb were left behind.

One by one the villagers squeezed through the small opening into a tunnel.

"This is a new tunnel," Danny whispered to Chip. "This must be a secret passage to somewhere in the Grandmaster's cavern."

"Do you think we'll see Melinda when we get there?" Chip asked while crawling on his knees behind Danny.

"Quiet," Danny whispered. Danny and Chip had decided to make their escape during the confusion of the battle. They would first look for Melinda, but if they couldn't find her, they would try to escape on their own and then return with a search party to rescue her.

The villagers snaked their way through the tunnel for an hour until they were ordered to stop. Then they were instructed to keep silent and move slowly out of the passage. Danny and Chip followed. They found themselves jammed with the other villagers into a cavern. Ralph whispered his orders. His face was lit by a flashlight that Harold held underneath him. The light cast deep shadows across Ralph's face.

"Behind this stone is a tunnel into Grandmaster Frank's headquarters. Our scouts have told us that the Grandmaster and most of his guardians should be asleep now. This is our chance to capture the Grandmaster and in doing so control our fate. We cannot fail. We cannot be afraid."

When he concluded, he motioned Harold and a few other men to move away a large stone. The villagers began entering the lair of Grandmaster Frank.

Chapter 25

Danny and Chip clutched their baseball bats as they entered the headquarters of Grandmaster Frank. Ahead in the darkness they could hear chaotic shouts. The Grandmaster's guardians had been surprised. Ralph's advance party had captured a few guardians who were sleeping in their chambers and they had found the storage compartment for the guns. But Danny and Chip both knew that there were hundreds, maybe thousands, of guardians ready to fight back. And they wondered how the Grandmaster's loyal followers would react to the invasion. Would they fight? Or would they see this as a chance to break free of the dominance of the Grandmaster?

Danny and Chip learned quickly that the guardians would put up a spirited fight. They entered a large courtyard in the center of one of the guardians' main barracks. Harold was leading a group of attackers who carried pipes, pitchforks, wooden beams, and shovels. Harold's squad swung their weapons furiously against a squad of guardians, who were stunned by the ferocity of the assault. Danny and Chip could hear the sounds of bone cracking. They could see on the stone floor pools of blood reflecting the soft light of the gas lanterns that hung in the doorways.

There were small skirmishes occurring all around them. But they did not want to fight. They were looking for an escape route. No one paid attention to what they were doing or seemed to care. People were fighting without any directions. No one was in command.

"Let's head toward that arch," Danny said, pointing to an exit on the far end of the courtyard. "Maybe it leads to the village."

"But what if someone sees us?" Chip said.

"Who would know if were part of Ralph's army or the Grandmaster's? This is the chance we've been waiting for."

"And will we try to find Melinda?" Chip inquired.

"We'll keep our eyes open, but we have to try to get out ourselves," Danny said. "Let's go."

They sprinted past the scattered clusters of people battling to the arched exit. One of the guardians leapt from the shadows and grabbed Danny by the neck, hoisting him off the ground in one sharp movement. Chip quickly swung his baseball bat at the guardian's knees, sending him crashing to the ground in agony. Danny lay sprawled next to the guardian, coughing and holding his throat.

"Danny, are you OK?" Chip said.

"Yes. Let's go," Danny said. He and Chip jumped over the wounded guardian and pushed open the barracks's door. They found themselves at the top of a very steep stone staircase that descended into the Grandmaster's city.

They could see fires burning and smoke beginning to ascend to the top of the immense cavern in which the town sat. They could also hear screaming drifting up from below.

"Let's go down and look for Melinda, but let's stay hidden in alleys if we can," Danny said.

They carefully descended into town through smoke that was becoming denser. They both began to cough and rub their eyes, which had begun to burn from the smoke and cinders in the air.

They hid in an alley that ran parallel to the main square. They were shocked at what they saw. Grandmaster Frank's own citizens were throwing stones at the guardians, who were on their way to reinforce the Grandmaster's fortress. The citizens were also setting fire to their own homes. Danny knew that they had to find Melinda soon before everyone was suffocated in the cavern.

Then through the smokey haze they spotted Arturis and the other creatures from the lake arising from the underground stream that flowed through the Grandmaster's city. The creatures joined in the battle against the Grandmaster's guardians. Ralph's troops let out a giant cheer as Arturis snatched a guardian in his menacing jaws and flung him against the rocks. With the lake creatures as their allies, Renegade Ralph's troops began to rout the fabled guardians of the Grandmaster.

Chapter 26

Amid the chaos of the fighting and the thickening smoke, Mother Mercedes was urging her children to defend the Grandmaster.

"Fight for our master! Protect him for all of the good he has given you!" she screamed.

Melinda saw the chaos as an opportunity to flee from Mother Mercedes. She talked to Clara and a few others, who agreed to lead the revolt. They crept up behind Mother Mercedes as she was hurling orders and insults at the children. Clara hit her over the head with a large wooden pole. A boy named Nate poked her hard in the ribs with a broom handle.

Mother Mercedes crumpled to the ground screaming in pain. The boy who had poked her yelled: "Hey everybody. Look. We've got her. We've finally got her! The old bitty!"

Some of the children who were fighting against Renegade Ralph's forces stopped and began to circle the fallen Mother Mercedes. They began spitting on her and kicking her. Mother Mercedes screamed and moaned, but the children would not stop tormenting her.

Melinda watched the ambush. She saw the children torturing Mother Mercedes. She suddenly became sick to her stomach.

"Stop this right now!" she yelled, as she began pushing the children away from Mother Mercedes. "You can't do this. You can't kill her."

"Why not?" said Nate, the boy who first hit Mother Mercedes.

"She was always yelling at us. Not giving us enough food or clothes. Hitting us. You want her dead as much as we do."

"Yeah. She hit us," some children chimed in.

"Kill her. Kill her," others chanted.

"But what you're doing is wrong. You're just as bad as she is if you keep hitting her," Melinda said.

"She doesn't deserve to live," a girl said.

"Look," Melinda said. "You've beaten her up. You've hurt her. Now this is your chance to escape from her. To get out of this place. Just go. Go!"

"Fine," Nate said. "You take care of her if you want to. I'm getting out of here. Let's go."

With a few final kicks and spits directed towards Mother Mercedes, the children, who for so long knew nothing except Mother Mercedes' scowl and anger, were free to leave. Mother Mercedes was beaten. They began to scatter and disappear into the smokey street battle.

Melinda was left alone with Mother Mercedes, whose face was bruised and bleeding.

"Why did you do it?" Mother Mercedes asked.

"Do what?"

"Help me."

"Because they would have killed you," Melinda said, helping Mother Mercedes stand up. "No matter how mean or cruel you were, you don't deserve to die."

"Do you think I was mean and cruel?" Mother Mercedes inquired.

"Yes. You never gave those boys and girls enough to eat. They were always cold. And you forced them to steal things from the place where I live. You're not very nice. My Grandmother is old, but she's nice. You're not," Melinda said.

"So you like your Grandmother," Mother Mercedes said.

"Yes. She tells me nice stories and takes me to her house in the country where there's lot of fresh air and animals," Melinda said.

"That sounds nice," Mother Mercedes said, brushing the dirt

from her clothes and wiping the blood off her face with a rag that she pulled out of her ripped jacket.

"We have to get out of here," Melinda said. "The smoke is getting thicker." Melinda then heard a faint yell coming from somewhere in the distance. It sounded like her name. It sounded like Danny.

"Danny!" she yelled. "Danny. I'm over here!" The voice grew louder and closer. Suddenly Danny and Chip emerged from the swirling smoke. Their faces were covered with soot. They were coughing. Melinda ran to them.

"Well, it's about time you got here. It's only been forty days. I can't count on you for anything," Melinda said, her hands on her hips. "Your hair is long and dirty and you're stinky."

"You don't look so pretty yourself," Danny replied.

"You guys can trade insults later. Let's just get out of here," Chip said.

Melinda turned to Mother Mercedes. "Can you show us the tunnel out of here?"

"It would be against the Grandmaster's rule," Mother Mercedes responded.

"But this place is being destroyed. It's burning," Melinda said. "Everyone will die, including you. You can escape, too."

"You did help me," Mother Mercedes said softly. "But I cannot come with you. My place is here. No matter what."

"But please show us the way home," Melinda said. "Hurry."

"Follow me," Mother Mercedes said, after bowing her head in thought. Danny, Chip, and Melinda followed Mother Mercedes into the smoke and darkness.

Chapter 27

Mother Mercedes guided Danny, Chip, and Melinda back to the large room where Melinda and the other children had slept. She grabbed a lantern and instructed them to follow her through the back alleys of the Grandmaster's village. From the smokey shadows, they could hear the screams and the fighting coming from all corners of the village.

Mother Mercedes led them through a dizzying maze of alleyways and narrow ascents until they were on a ledge high in the cavern. The village below was shrouded completely in smoke. They stopped for only a second to look.

They then crawled into a small passage that headed upward. Mother Mercedes kept a fast pace ahead of them, urging them to hurry.

Their knees and backs ached as they furiously followed Mother Mercedes. They could feel warm air flowing down the passageway. They were nearing the top.

"Stop right here," Mother Mercedes ordered. They were crammed into a small chamber. "This is as far as I can take you. Continue climbing a few more feet and you will be back in your world."

"Are you coming with us?" Melinda asked.

"I cannot. I must return to where I belong. People in your world don't understand us," Mother Mercedes said.

"But maybe you should let people try," Danny said.

"I would like to share your optimism. But I'm too old. I must return to serve the Grandmaster. Go, and don't come back," Mother Mercedes said as she headed back down the passage. Her lantern light was swallowed in the darkness.

"Thank you," Danny, Chip, and Melinda yelled. Their voices echoed against the rock walls. Mother Mercedes did not respond. She was gone.

"So what are we waiting for? Let's go," Chip said. They all scrambled quickly up the passage, emerging in a city dump outside of town.

Even though it was twilight, their eyes had a hard time adjusting to the faint light. They kept their heads down and away from the setting sun. It was a hot and muggy night, and they all took deep gulps of the summer air. They didn't even mind that it smelled like rotting garbage.

"Do you know where we are?" Chip asked.

"Yes, we're about two miles west of town," Danny said. "I remember the location from my map of Rivertown. Follow me."

As bats swirled over their heads looking for insects, a full moon rose over the trees. They were finally going home.

Chapter 28

The next afternoon this article appeared on the front page of the Rivertown Register:

Three Missing Children Suddenly Reappear

Three Rivertown children reappeared last night after having mysteriously disappeared forty days ago. Patrolling the west side of town along Carter Road near the municipal landfill, police officer Frank Wembley was flagged down by Danny Boyle, who was walking on the side of the road with his sister Melinda and a friend Chip Zumhoffer. The three children identified themselves to Officer Wembley and asked to be taken home.

"The children were covered with mud and soot and were wearing filthy, torn clothes. But otherwise they were fine" said Officer Wembley, who took the children immediately to the emergency room at Roosevelt Hospital, where they remain under observation. They will undergo a series of physical and psychological examinations before being released to their parents, said a hospital spokesperson.

Police commissioner Stan Fredericks said that the Boyles and Zumhoffers had met with their children and were relieved and thankful that the children were found alive. The commissioner declined to answer any questions regarding the ongoing investigation into the children's disappearance or whether an arrest was imminent for the person or persons who might have abducted the children.

"All I can say is that we have interviewed each of the children. We are following up on their stories," said Commissioner Fredericks.

A police source, however, has informed the *Rivertown Register* that the children told the police they had spent the past forty days in an underground city far beneath Rivertown. According to their story, the inhabitants of the underground city were responsible for the series of mysterious home collapses that have been occurring in Rivertown.

Nan Burrows, a child psychologist at Rivertown College, explained that fanciful stories of mysterious worlds can be a sign that the children suffered a severe traumatic episode. "Not wanting to deal with the real pain of their ordeal, whatever that might have been, the children have concocted a story that helps them come to terms with the trauma," she said. "It's likely that they are speaking in some kind of code that will be deciphered through professional counseling and with the support of their families. We all hope for the best for the children. They have obviously been through a lot."

In the days and weeks following their reappearance and reunion with their families, Danny, Melinda, and Chip were given a battery of tests and endured hours of interrogation by psychologists, police, and their parents. They were asked repeatedly to tell the truth. When they all said over and over again that they were telling the truth, their interrogators grew more angry and frustrated.

Finally, their parents stepped in and told the authorities to leave their children alone. Neither Danny nor Melinda nor Chip had been harmed physically, and the police could not find any evidence of a crime, so finally the interview sessions ended.

Secretly, however, police commissioner Fredericks ordered a search of the cave into which the children had originally entered. No evidence of an underground city was ever found. The case remains open, but no investigators are currently assigned to it.

Danny and Chip spent the rest of the summer staying close to home. Danny, however, visited Uncle Albert regularly to give him the details of his stay in the underland. Uncle Albert sat in his undershirt, sipped his beer, and asked Danny dozens of questions. He was pleased that Danny was safe but also surprised that the tale of the underland was actually true. Uncle Albert never confessed to Danny that he thought the story had only been a tall tale, a legend for old timers like him to tell little children. But he believed Danny when other adults would not. He wished that he could go to the underland himself.

As their summer vacation grew shorter, Danny and Chip spent as much time as possible at their treehouse. They even invited Melinda along from time to time to read comic books with them.

As they climbed up to the roof hatch one hot afternoon late in August, just a few days before school was to begin, they saw that a piece of paper had been nailed to the tree trunk.

"Great," Danny said, "someone found our treehouse."

"I bet it was Joey Becker. I bet he trashed the inside, too," Chip said.

"Well, are you going to read the note or should I?" Melinda said impatiently.

"I'll read it," Danny said, ripping the paper off from the trunk. He read the note silently.

"Well, what does Joey have to say?" Joey said.

"Look," Danny said, handing the note to Chip. "Read for yourself. It's from Harold. He says everyone in Renegade Ralph's village misses us. He knows where he can find us, and that we may hear from him again soon. Isn't that great!"

Chip and Melinda looked at each other as if to say: "Here we go again."

The End (Or Just A New Beginning?)

ABOUT THE AUTHOR

William Graham is a graduate of Northwestern University. He and his wife Jacqueline live in Chicago, Illinois.

ABOUT GREATUNPUBLISHED.COM

greatunpublished.com is a website that exists to serve writers and readers, and remove some of the commercial barriers between them. When you purchase a greatunpublished.com title, whether you receive it in electronic form or in a paperback volume or as a signed copy of the author's manuscript, you can be assured that the author is receiving a majority of the post-production revenue. Writers who join greatunpublished.com support the site and its marketing efforts with a per-title fee, and a portion of the site's share of profits are channeled into literacy programs.

So by purchasing this title from greatunpublished.com, you are helping to revolutionize the publishing industry for the benefit of writers and readers.
And for this we thank you.